WE BOTH READ®

Parent's Introduction

We Both Read is the first series of books designed to invite parents and children to share the reading of a story by taking turns reading aloud. This "shared reading" innovation, which was developed with reading education specialists, invites parents to read the more complex text and storyline on the left-hand pages. Children are encouraged to read the right-hand pages, which feature less complex text and storyline, specifically written for the beginning reader. You will note that a "talking parent" icon ☺ precedes the parent's text and a "talking child" icon ☺ precedes the child's text.

Reading aloud is one of the most important activities parents can share with their child to assist them in their reading development. However, *We Both Read* goes beyond reading **to** a child and allows parents to share the reading **with** a child. *We Both Read* is so powerful and effective because it combines two key elements in learning: "modeling" (the parent reads) and "doing" (the child reads). The result is not only faster reading development for the child, but a much more enjoyable and enriching experience for both!

You may find it helpful to read the entire book aloud yourself the first time, then invite your child to participate in the second reading. We encourage you to share and interact with your child as you read the book together. If your child is having difficulty, you might want to mention a few things to help them. "Sounding out" is good, but it will not work with all words. They can pick up clues about the words they are reading from the story, the context of the sentence, or even the pictures. Some stories have rhyming patterns that might help. For beginning readers, you also might want to suggest touching the words with their finger as they read, so they can better connect the voice sound and the printed word.

Sharing the *We Both Read* books together will engage you and your child in an interactive adventure in reading! It is a fun and easy way to encourage and help your child to read—and a wonderful way to start them off on a lifetime of reading enjoyment!

We Both Read: Lulu's Lost Shoes

—————————————————

Text Copyright ©2004 by Paula Blankenship
Illustrations Copyright ©2004 by Larry Reinhart
All rights reserved

We Both Read® is a trademark of Treasure Bay, Inc.

Published by Treasure Bay, Inc.
17 Parkgrove Drive
South San Francisco, CA 94080 USA

PRINTED IN SINGAPORE

Library of Congress Catalog Card Number: 2004100571

Hardcover ISBN: 1-891327-55-0
Paperback ISBN: 1-891327-56-9

FIRST EDITION

We Both Read® Books
Patent No. 5,957,693

Visit us online at:
www.webothread.com

WE BOTH READ®

Lulu's Lost Shoes

By Paula Blankenship

Illustrated by Larry Reinhart

TREASURE BAY

Morning shines in upon Lulu.
It shines on her little pet, Fred.
She wakes and she yawns and she stretches.
Then Lulu jumps up from . . .

. . . her bed.

Lulu heads down to the kitchen.
She flutters and flitters and dips.
She flies past her mom, who is cooking,
And into her chair . . .

. . . Lulu flips.

Mother says, "Lulu, stop playing.
Your breakfast is starting to cool!
And time's flying faster than you are.
Please hurry and head off . . .

. . . to school."

Nibbles and burps and "Excuse me!"
Then breakfast is finally done.
Her backpack and lunch are both waiting.
Now Lulu is ready . . .

. . . to run.

"Hold it!" calls Dad from his garden.
"Your feet are all wiggling free.
Go put on your shoes before leaving!
I saw them last night by . . .

. . . the tree."

Lulu looks under the willow.
Now where in the world could they be?
She asks her pet, Fred, "Have you seen them?"
But he shrugs, saying, "Don't look . . .

. . . at me."

Lulu flies up to a beehive.
The bees may give Lulu some clues!
They're friendly and they can be helpful.
But they haven't seen . . .

. . . Lulu's shoes.

Lulu runs down to the water.
Her shoes may have dropped in the creek!
"Barrump," says a frog, "I can help you.
Just wait while I go take . . .

. . . a peek."

Frog tries his best, but can't find them.
There's nothing left here to discuss.
Poor Lulu's bare feet are still shoeless
And here comes the big . . .

. . . yellow bus.

"Where are my shoes?!" Lulu wonders.
"I know they're not under the tree.
I know they're not up in the beehive.
My shoes must be hiding . . .

. . . from
me!"

Up bumps the bus in the driveway.
The driver is given the news.
Then Mother Bug asks, "Can you wait here,
Until we can . . .

. . . find Lulu's shoes?"

Spiders and bugs are not patient,
Or quiet or sweet like a mouse.
They like to be flitting and flying!
And so they invade . . .

. . . Lulu's house!

Insects are helpful by nature.
They all want to help Lulu look.
They peer behind bookshelves and lampshades
To search every light bulb . . .

. . . and book.

Into the house leap the crickets.
The grasshoppers hop down the hall.
The spiders explore every bedroom.
The beetles have found . . .

. . . Lulu's ball.

Butterflies swing on the curtains.
The moths find a vacuum to use.
The stinkbugs explore every trash can.
But no one has found . . .

. . . Lulu's shoes.

Mother is not very happy.
Now EVERYONE here will be late!
And all of the shoes are still missing.
The only thing found . . .

. . . is a skate.

Lifting the couch is a termite,
A curious, strong little bug.
She carefully searches beneath it,
While others look . . .

. . . under the rug.

Lulu has looked through the garden.
She's tired and flushed from the heat.
So all of her friends crowd around her
And tickle her shoeless . . .

. . . bug feet.

Mother comes in and they tell her
They've searched every cranny and nook!
Then Mother says, "Peek in your closet.
It's always the last place . . .

. . . you look."

Suddenly shoes fall around them.
They just can't believe the good news!
And everyone bursts out with laughter,
"At last we have found . . .

. . . Lulu's shoes!"

If you liked **Lulu's Lost Shoes**, here are two other We Both Read® Books you are sure to enjoy!

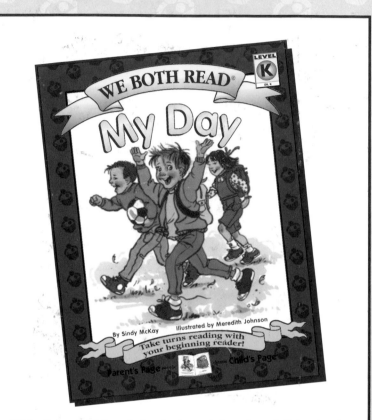

This Level K book is designed for the child who is just being introduced to reading. The child's pages have only one or two words, which relate directly to the illustration and even rhyme with what has just been read to them. This title is a charming story about what a child does in the course of a simple happy day.